THE REMA

CHRONICLES

REALM OF THE BLUE MIST

Library of Congress Control Number: 2021937052

ISBN 978-1-338-11515-4 (hardcover)
ISBN 978-1-338-11513-0 (paperback)

10 9 8 7 6 5 4 3 2 1   22 23 24 25 26

Printed in China   62
First edition, March 2022

Edited by Cassandra Pelham Fulton
Creative Director: Phil Falco
Publisher: David Saylor

AMY KIM KIBUISHI

THE REMA
CHRONICLES

BOOK ONE
REALM OF THE BLUE MIST

graphix

AN IMPRINT OF

■Scholastic

PART I
HAUNTED

The wind.

The trees.

The birds.

They sound like voices.

If I close my eyes...

I can almost understand them.

SPLORCH!

hff! hff! hff!

hff! hff!

5

The day I finally meet the ghost woman.

I was eight years old when I first saw her.

My father was the lab director at a place called PSPR -- Pike State Park Research.

PSPR's purpose to stud mist le fro Yggdr

The mist was reported to give everlasting life...

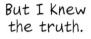

But I knew the truth.

It didn't let you die. It kept you alive, forever aging.

Dad's lab was full of specimens from the woods -- squirrels that were more mummy than animal.

But it never affected humans.

At least, not until the ghost.

I was playing near Dad's lab when I heard his voice.

Or some thing.

He died a week later.

I found his body where we always met -- beneath Yggdrasil.

The autopsy said his brain correlated with his time of death, but his body had aged two hundred years.

He was the first and only human victim of Yggdrasil's mist.

The lab was shut down. The site was labeled a biohazard.

The town erased PSPR from its memory and quickly buried what happened.

Mom forbade me to enter the woods...

But I went anyway.

No one dared set foot in the woods anymore, so it became my sanctuary.

A place [where I] could b[e] myself.

Because when you grow up with five-eyed crows and undead squirrels, you Kind of need a sanctuary.

poke

And I guess part of me understood that it wasn't the woods that Killed my dad. Or the mist.

It was the ghost.

Mom said the ghost was[n't] real, but I Knew. I saw [her] myself, and Dad Kept draw[ing] of her hidden in his lat[er]

Lots of them.

She took my dad away for some reason. I needed to know why.

I hiked to Yggdrasil every day after school, looking for her.

I would lie down where I found Dad's body...

And wai͏ hoping to mee͏ the ghost.

For seven years, she never came.

Then one crisp autumn day, shortly after I turned fifteen, the ghost finally took me away.

The boy
with blue
hair.

If I think about
you instead of
the ghost...

SHHH

SHHHWW

Our handsome voyager, back in one piece! You seem pale, Philip. Are you all right?

I'm fine. It's good to see your smile again, Lina.

A girlfriend?

So. How much have you collected?

More than enough.

Good. That'll keep the Council happy!

General Raed's waiting at Keeper Central with Sofen and the rest of the Council. If we get there quickly, we can hit Paeter's place afterward and celebrate!

Count me out. I'm retiring early. Interplanetary travel can be taxing.

Interplanetary?

Maybe it's code for something.

Aw. Are you sure?

Sorry, Lina. Perhaps later.

We'd better get going.

We...
We're
flying!

W-wait...

Is that a
planet?!

Philip, we're
not on Earth?

No, we
are not!

We're not
on Earth...!

There!

PART II
GEIST

SSSSSHHHHHH

Cyphr, born from light, gravity, and electricity, he is the God of Forces.

Felaxx, born from lava, fire, and heat, she is the Goddess of Fire.

Merofi, born from water, mist, and rain, she is the Goddess of Water.

Gratiat, born of wind, air, and clouds, he is the God of Wind.

And Rema, born from rock and soil, she is the Goddess of Stone and Green Life.

And Cyphr in sparks across the world with his fatherly pride, giving us light.

The world was beautiful, but soon The Gods became lonely. They decided to create people to populate Rema.

So Rema made people with her hair.

Cyphr made people with his sparks.

Felaxx made people with the fire in her heart.

Merofi made people with her tears.

And Gratiat made people with his freedom.

The people had godlike powers, able to summon water, fire, wind, light, and rock at their bidding. They were beautiful but corrupt. They hungered to be as powerful as The Gods who created them.

While The Gods slept, the people tapped into their veins and harvested their blood, spilling it over the land until it became part of the ground. The people drew the blood of The Gods at their whim and shaped the world as they pleased. They named this power "ciphrony" after Cyphr, the most powerful of The Gods.

The Gods did not take this lightly. Enraged, Cyphr set a curse on all who dared to use their blood for power. From then on, ciphrony corrupted the souls of the people, until they became possessed by it.

The more ciphrony they used, the more they craved, until entire nations destroyed themselves to obtain it. The people became mindless vessels that wandered the world like ghosts, flooding and burning everything in their paths. Thus, The Gods named them "geists."

Fearing complete destruction of all they had built,
The Five Holy Gods banded together and destroyed
every geist they could find. All trace of the people
was wiped from Rema's surface. The land was quiet
for many eons after.

As the silent ages passed, The Gods
became lonely once more.

Merofi wanted to make new
people. Cyphr, in his wisdom,
reminded the others of the geists.
They could not let pride get in
the way of their creations. If they
were to make new people, they
must use their hair, sparks, heart,
tears, and freedom all together,
as one.

The other Gods agreed and
they created a harmonious
people -- good, humble, and
harmless. The balanced people
were kind and spent their days
worshipping The Gods in peace.
Finally, The Five Holy Gods had
created a world they could
share without fear, greed,
or spite.

The Gods were so pleased, they made enough balanced people to fill a country. Then, overjoyed, enough to fill the world.

As they made more and more balanced people, filling the world with life and laughter, they unwittingly conjured an occasional geist. These geists were identical to the corrupt spirits from ages past. They were powerful, beautiful, and helplessly addicted to ciphrony, the blood of The Gods.

Ciphrony gave them memories that reached through Time. The geists remembered how The Gods gave them life. More than this, they remembered how The Gods took it away. They wanted to destroy The Gods and their people. They wanted to make them feel the pain they suffered so long ago.

Thus the ancient feud between geist and non-geist began. The geists walk amongst the balanced people, always in hiding and always hungry for ciphrony.

Let it be remembered to Remans past, present, and future. The balanced ones are the chosen people of Rema, chosen by The Gods.

This is how Rema came to life. The Five Holy Gods are the ones who gave it to us. The geists are the ones who want to take it away. The geists are the ones who want us dead.

So many Merofi's Tears.

Do they believe geists are evil, like the Remanora?

PART III
THE PRIESTESS

187

He's a good person -- patient, dedicated, brave.

He's not the emotionless soldier he pretends to be.

I wonder if he'll ever see that. It's kind of sad...I'll never find out.

I have everything I need.

My clothes, my book...

And the Earth Key.

The marina isn't far. I'll borrow a boat and row to the Portal Atrium.

I've been lost on Rema long enough.

Time to go home.

209

Ah, General Raed. You're just in time.

These two are fugitives. Shockingly, one is an alien from the neutral world, Earth.

I don't know how she got here, but I can assure you --

You had no right to capture her.

With respect, General, I am the Grand Merofian Priestess. Under Merofi's guidance, I capture whoever I deem a threat.

With respect, Hiida, I doubt Merofi guides those who ignore her city's laws.

Interplanetary matters belong to the Council and the Keepers.

Your actions show disregard for both. You are under Keeper surveillance from now on, by command of Helvir Law!

PART IV
THE GHOST

So...

Who will house the girl as a permanent resident?

SHK

What?

She will never go back to Earth. Therefore, I need to know where she will be living from now on.

All immigrants to Cerey must be logged into the citizens' roster. I'm happy to do that here.

I'm sorry, but...

Did you say I'm **never** going back to Earth?

That's right.

Earth's sun?

Yes.

I learned long ago, no matter how far you travel, home has a way of finding you.

You may be stranded here, but you are not alone. If you ever need to talk, to remember Earth...let me know.

I'll be inside. When you're ready, I can deliver your farewell letter.

Okay...

Tabetha Simon...

At last, we speak.

What do you want from me?!

Use your inner voice.

The Gods of Rema are listening, and they cannot know I am here.

He was trying to avoid the inevitable -- that you would come here and discover his work.

He learned the hard way, however, that there is no avoiding fate.

Your father's ambition consumed him. I **had** to let him die...

I will not ask your forgiveness, but in time, perhaps your understanding. I had no choice.

What's **so** important that you'd sacrifice my father's life and risk mine?

This city is an old place full of dark secrets, Tabetha Simon.

I brought you here to find that darkness, and **illuminate** it.

What do you mean?

...Your father was not the man you thought he was.

TO BE CONTINUED

Don't miss the next book in Tabby's adventure.
Here's a sneak peek . . .

THE REMA CHRONICLES

BOOK TWO
KINGDOM OF WATER

PART I
THE LETTER

ACKNOWLEDGMENTS

Rema has been a sanctuary through many phases of my life — as a teen struggling with family hardships, as a post-college graduate searching for my voice, and as a mother of young children finding peace in the chaos. So many friends, family, mentors, and online readers had an impact on this story. Thanking everyone would be impossible, so if you ever encountered The Rema Chronicles as a webcomic, zine, or online novel — you were the distant voices cheering this project on. My first thanks are to you.

Key people understood this story better than I did at times. One is Jen Lee Quick, who, when we met in college, recommended I turn my scattered drawings of Rema into a comic, and who always knew exactly what to say to inspire me to keep going. Another is Maurene Goo, who read my broken prose more times than I can count yet was still excited to see what happened next.

This book wouldn't be possible without my family: my beautiful mother and my hero, Sun Hui Kim, my brother, Tim Ganter, who always believed in Rema no matter what, and my two sweet children — thank you for keeping me grounded as I worked.

Thank you to my editor, Cassandra Pelham Fulton, who helped usher this project onto the public stage in a way I never thought possible, to David Saylor for his steadfast support, to Phil Falco for his keen eye, and to everyone at Scholastic who had a hand in finalizing the book. Rema couldn't have asked for a better home.

These pages wouldn't look nearly as good without the many hours of coloring assistance from Emmy Toyonaga and especially Audra Furuichi, who has repeatedly gone above and beyond for Rema. I couldn't have finished this book without either of your help and good company. To my incredible agent, Judy Hansen, you have been through so much with this project. I truly couldn't have done this without your wisdom, hard truths, and positive attitude.

My biggest, most heartfelt thanks are reserved for my dear husband, Kazu Kibuishi. My coach, my harshest critic, and my biggest cheerleader — your undying faith in me and this project, and your vision for what it could be, has never wavered. I love you with all my heart and soul. This book is for you.

ABOUT THE AUTHOR

Amy Kim Kibuishi has been drawing and writing in earnest since she was ten years old. She graduated from the School of Visual Arts with a degree in Cartooning and is the creator of Sorcerers & Secretaries, a graphic novel duology. The first volume was a YALSA Great Graphic Novels for Teens selection. She was also a contributor to the acclaimed Flight anthology series edited by Kazu Kibuishi, and adapted a story for *Goosebumps: Terror Trips* by R.L. Stine. Amy lives in Washington State with her husband, Kazu, and their two children.

CREATED AT

WITH COLOR ASSISTANCE BY
AUDRA FURUICHI
EMMY TOYONAGA

PAGE FLATTING BY
AUDRA FURUICHI